The Snooze Brothers

By Cindy Kenney and Doug Peterson
Illustrated by Michael Moore

bigidea.com

ZONDERVAN.com/
AUTHORTRACKER
follow your favorite authors

ZONDERKIDZ

The Snooze Brothers
Copyright© 2005 Big Idea Entertainment, LLC. VEGGIETALES®, character names,
likenesses and other indicia are trademarks of and copyrighted by Big Idea
Entertainment, LLC.

Requests for information should be addressed to:

Zondervan, *Grand Rapids, Michigan 49530*

Library of Congress Cataloging-in-Publication Data

Kenney, Cindy, 1959–
     The snooze brothers / by Cindy Kenney and Doug Peterson.
        p.   cm. — (VeggieTown values ; bk 6).
     Summary: Junior and Laura lose track of Lil' Pea while babysitting, then
get a lesson in responsibility when a book transports them into the middle of a
car chase that is not what it seems to be.
     ISBN 978-0-310-70739-4 (softcover)
     [1. Responsibility — Fiction. 2. Babysitters — Fiction. 3. Conduct of life —
Fiction. 4. Vegetables — Fiction.] I. Peterson, Doug. II. Title. III. Series.
PZ7.K3933Sno 2006
[Fic — dc22.   2005025154

Written by: Cindy Kenney & Doug Peterson
Illustrated by: Michael Moore
Editor: Amy DeVries
Art direction & design: Karen Poth

Printed in Hong Kong

10 11 12 13 14 15 16 17 /PEH/ 22 21 20 19 18 17 16 15 14 13 12 11 10 9 8 7 6 5 4

"Work as if you were not serving people but the Lord."
(Ephesians 6:7)

Junior Asparagus and Laura Carrot were pooped!

Babysitting wasn't easy. Li'l Pea started the morning by making mud pies on his mother's good dishes. And when Laura and Junior tried to stop him, he slung mud all over the house! After that, Junior and Laura decided they needed a break while Li'l Pea played outside.

Only one problem. Li'l Pea spotted a grasshopper. He followed it to the front of the house . . .

. . . then to the curb.

. . . and finally into the street.

Tires squealed.

Li'l Pea (and the grasshopper) hopped back in the nick of time. Whew! He was safe. But Junior and Laura were in a heap of trouble. Junior's parents were driving the car.

"Your job was to watch Li'l Pea," Junior's dad said sternly.
Junior and Laura begged for another chance.

"Not until you're able to show more responsibility." Mr. Asparagus said as he shook his head. "Being responsible means working with all your heart. You should work as if you are serving God."

Later that day, Junior and Laura visited the Treasure Trove Bookstore.

"I have just the book for you," Mr. O'Malley said. "It's somewhere in the 'Responsibility section'."

"Aye, here it is. *The Snooze Brothers.*"

"This book is about two brothers who need help," he said with a wink. "And helping them will be a true mission from God."

ONCE UPON A TIME

As Junior opened the book, four giant words floated up from inside the cover. Four simple words: Once Upon A Time...

"Wait!" Mr. O'Malley shouted. "I've got to tell you something! The Snooze Brothers are...!"

WHOOOOOOOOOOOOSH!

Too late.

The words swirled around. Junior and Laura tumbled **over**
        and over
           and over...
              and landed in a huge busy city.

Two Veggies tore down an alley, scared out of their gourds. "Help! Save us!" one of them yelled.

"What's taking the Snooze-Mobile so long?"

Junior and Laura looked at one another. "The Snooze Brothers!"

Just then a car squealed around the corner and skidded to a stop.
Junior, Laura, and the Snooze Brothers dove into the back seat and landed in
a pile of...pillows!? The Snooze Brothers quickly snuggled in and fell asleep.

As the car sped away, the driver turned around and greeted his new passengers. "Hi! I'm Larry the Cucumber. Those two are Joliet Jammies and Snoreman Snooze. You can call them the Snooze Brothers."

"Are they in trouble?" asked Laura.

Larry pointed behind them. "Look!"

Out the rear window Junior and Laura saw cars racing after them. The drivers all had brown cases.

Junior gasped. "I bet they're hiding weapons in those cases!"

"This must be our mission from God," Laura said. "It's our responsibility to save the Snooze Brothers."

Larry grinned. "Load up the Pillow-Blaster!"

Suddenly a hatch sprung open in the roof of the car.

"Load the blaster with pillows and start firing!" shouted Larry.

Ka-pow! Whop!

Pillows smashed against the bad guys' cars. Soon the air filled with feathers.

"I want my blankie," murmured Joliet Jammies as he slept.

Things got worse. Mushrooms riding motorcycles joined the chase. They all had cases strapped to their backs.

"More pillows!" cried Junior.

Ka-pow! Zing!

Pillow after pillow zipped through the air.

"Look out!" yelled Laura.

A helicopter zoomed in.

Soon, scooters, skateboards, and pogo sticks were after them.

"Who are these guys?" asked Laura.

"Uh-oh," said Larry. "I hope you can swim."

Larry slammed on the brakes. The car skidded and spun and came to a stop inches from a lake.

The "bad guys" surrounded the Snooze-Mobile.

"We're goners!" moaned Larry.

"Not so fast!" said a little old mushroom. She jumped off her motorcycle and opened her case.

"Watch out!" Junior shouted. "She's going for her weapon!"

Ma Mushroom frowned. "Are you calling my saxophone a weapon?"

Then all of the Veggies opened their cases. They pulled out tubas, trombones, clarinets, and more.

Laura gasped. "Musical instruments! We thought you were bad guys!"

Ma Mushroom sighed. "We're musicians, not bad guys. We play the blues. The Snooze Brothers are the leaders of our band, and we're trying to get them to the church. Our show goes on in five minutes!"

"We thought the Snooze Brothers were in trouble," Laura said. "We were trying to help them."

"If you want to help, get them to the church on time," said Ma Mushroom. "Joliet Jammies and Snoreman are always running away from responsibility. The only thing they work hard at is sleeping."

Responsibility. Junior's dad used that word. It meant working with your whole heart.

"This concert will raise money to save our church!" exclaimed Ma Mushroom.

"So *this* must be our mission from God," Junior said. "Larry, can you get us to the church in five minutes?"

"No problem, boss."

"I'll lead the way!" chimed Police Officer Scooter.

Like a huge parade, the Snooze-Mobile raced behind the police car, followed by motorcycles, skateboards, and scooters.

On the way, Junior and Laura worked hard to wake the Snooze Brothers. "Sleep later," Junior said. "Right now you gotta be responsible."

The two sleepy gourds finally agreed to do their very best on stage. The crowd at the church went wild. They all sang, "Re-spon-si-bil-i-ty!, Find out what it means to me! Ohhhhhh, sock it to me, sock it to me, sock it to me..."

    As the Snooze Brothers played their last song, balloons and confetti rained down. The money they earned saved the church.

    Mixed in with the balloons were two large words: **THE END**.

    "I guess it's time for us to go," Junior said sadly.

    Joliet Jammies beamed. "Thanks for showing us how to be responsible!"

In the blink of an eye, Junior and Laura found themselves back in the bookstore.

"We did it, Mr. O'Malley! We saved the church!"

"Well done," said Mr. O'Malley. He put the "Closed" sign in the window. His hard work was over for the day.

"I can't wait to study up on babysitting," added Junior. "Do you have the books *Owies, Boo-Boos, and Other Medical Emergencies* and *101 Ways to Get Mud Off the Ceiling?* We're going to be the most responsible babysitters in town!"

"Shhh," Laura whispered. "Look."

Junior whispered, "We can tell him about it in the morning."

Laura tucked a blanket around the old potato. Junior placed a Teddy Bear next to him. They turned out the lights and slipped out the door.

Mr. O'Malley popped open one eye. He grinned, yawned, and returned to his nap.

Mission accomplished.